Tiptoe Into Kindergarten

by Jacqueline Rogers

A B C D E F G
CHALKBOARD
HEATER
SUPPLIES
RICE TABLE
BOOKS
TABLE
TABLE
CALENDAR AND WEATHER CENTER
OCTOBER
SUNNY
CLOUDY
RAINY
SNOWY
TEACHER'S DESK
TEACHER'S STUFF
Z Y X W

SINK
STORY CENTER
BATHROOM
CHALK BOARD
TABLE
COMPUTER
CUBBIES
CLASSROOM DOOR

Tiptoe Into Kindergarten

To the kindergarten teachers of the
M.E.D. Elementary School
—J.R.

Library of Congress Card Catalog Numbers: 98-45430
ISBN 0-439-48592-4

10 9 8 7 6 5 4 04 05 06 07

Printed in the U.S.A. 23
First trade paperback edition, June 2003

Tiptoe Into Kindergarten

by Jacqueline Rogers

SCHOLASTIC INC. Cartwheel BOOKS®
New York Toronto London Auckland Sydney
Mexico City New Delhi Hong Kong Buenos Aires

Tiptoe, tiptoe,
no one's looking

I can be
so very still

J K L M N O

SUNNY
OCTOBER
SUNDAY
MONDAY
TUESDAY
WEDNESDAY
THURSDAY
FRIDAY
1
2
3

Hiding, hiding,
I can watch now
what they're doing
all day long

First a big book—
what a BIG BOOK!
Yummy colors
I must touch

On the chalkboard
I make letters
Take my turn
when they are done

3
6

Now some block games
roll-big-dice games
I count numbers
1, 2, 3

Puzzles puzzles
I find places—
This will fit in here
somehow

Uh oh, uh oh,
got to go now—
Where's the bathroom?
over there

Washing hands
like Mommy tells me
Big kids do it, too,
I see

What's inside that
funny table?
Rice, they call it
I must try

Crawling crawling
I find cubbies
full of goody things
inside

HELEN
MARTIN
DAVID
KRISTIN
BOBBY
JONATHAN
GRACE
EDIE

Singing songs now
jumpy songs now
Clapping hands
and stomping feet

They eat snack
while I try smock on
Got to paint a
big fat sun

I feel sleepy—
Where is Mommy?
I'll curl up for
just a bit

What a nice place
sunny fun place
I'll be back
I hope real soon

a A b B c C d D e E f F g G
CHALKBOARD
HEATER
SUPPLIES
RICE TABLE
BOOKS
TABLE
TABLE
Z z
Y y
OCTOBER
CALENDAR AND WEATHER CENTER
SUNNY
CLOUDY
RAINY
SNOWY
X x
W w
TEACHER'S STUFF
TEACHER'S DESK
COATS

SINK
STORY CENTER
BATHROOM
CHALK BOARD
COMPUTER
CUBBIES
CLASSROOM DOOR